This igloo book belongs to:

....

Published in 2019
by Igloo Books Ltd
Cottage Farm
Sywell
NN6 0BJ
www.igloobooks.com

1019 002.01
2 4 6 8 10 9 7 5 3
ISBN 978-1-78905-193-3

Written by Melanie Joyce
Illustrated by Helen Rowe

Printed and manufactured in China

Goodnight, Little Bear

igloobooks

Little Bear was feeling sleepy. It was nearly the end of the day.
His mum had come to take him home. There was no more time to play.

Little Bear yawned and gave a stretch. "I feel a bit tired," he said.
Mum took his tiny paw in hers and gently stroked his head.

"All little bears get sleepy," said Mum, "and the sun is sinking low.
It will soon be bedtime for everyone. It's time for us to go."

Little Bear gave his mummy a cuddle, in the rosy evening light.
"Can I go to see my friends?" he asked. "I want to say goodnight."

Little Bear said goodnight to the birds, twittering in their nest.
They fluttered their wings and chirruped, then settled down to rest.

Mother Duck quacked to her ducklings and they cuddled under her wing.
"Goodnight," said Little Bear to them, as the skylark began to sing.

Mum and Little Bear went to the stream where all the fish swished.
Little Bear said goodnight to the frogs as they happily splashed and splished.

"I've had a lovely day," said Little Bear, "and it's been lots of fun. Goodnight," he said to the foal dozing under the setting sun.

"Goodnight," said Little Bear to the butterflies, fluttering in the breeze.

He said goodnight to the fluffy squirrels nestling in the trees.

"I wish you sweet dreams," said Little Bear to the sleepy, soft dormouse.

"Sleep tight," he said to the baby bunnies curled up in their cozy house.

Along the shadowy woodland paths, the meadow bees came humming. "They are flying back to their hive," said Mum, "because the night is coming."

"When will night be here?" said Little Bear. "Will it be coming soon?"
"Yes," replied Mum, "and then you will see the stars and shining moon."

Little Bear looked up into the sky and the glowing sun had gone.
In its place were twinkling stars and a round moon brightly shone.

"The stars are magic," said Little Bear and he gave a sleepy yawn.
Then he said goodnight to the dozing deer and the little fawn.

"Come on," said Mum. "It's getting late and you're a tired little bear."
Very gently, she scooped him up and softly said, "There, there."

Little Bear felt very tired. He gave his mummy a sleepy hug.
"We'll soon be home," said Mum, "and you'll be nice and snug."

Soon, Little Bear was safely home and ready to go to bed.
He chose a bedtime story and then he snuggled down with Ted.

Before the story was over, Little Bear's eyes began to close.
Mum just looked at him and smiled, then kissed his little nose.

At last, Little Bear was fast asleep and in the world of dreams.
His bedroom was filled with starlight and silvery, soft moonbeams.

"Goodnight, Little Bear," said Mum, "sleep safely through the night. I will watch over you and keep you safe until the morning light."

Goodnight, Little Bear. Sweet dreams.